Not another lie!

"Janie!" Alex shouted. "I've thought of a way to get new shoelaces!"

"You mean you're finally going to tell the truth?" Janie asked.

"No!" Alex explained. "If I buy new laces just like the old ones, Mom will never know I lost the old ones."

"Ridiculous!" Janie exclaimed. "New shoelaces always look cleaner than the old ones. And my mom would kill me if she knew I went to the store myself."

"She'll never know. Besides, you won't be by yourself," added Alex. "You'll be with me."

ALEX

Shoelaces and Brussels Sprouts

Nancy Simpson

Equipping Kids for Life

An Imprint of Cook Communications Ministries • Colorado Springs, CO

Faith Kidz® is an imprint of
Cook Communications Ministries
4050 Lee Vance View
Colorado springs, CO 80918
Cook Communications, Paris, Ontario
Kingsway Communications, Eastbourne, England

SHOELACES AND BRUSSELS SPROUTS

Cover design by Megan Keeane DeSantis
Cover illustration by Don Stewart

First printing, 1987
Printed in the United States of America
16 17 18 19 20 21 22 Printing/Year 08 07 06 05 04

Library of Congress Cataloging-in-Publication Data

Simpson, Nancy, 1949-
Shoelaces and Brussels sprouts
Summary: A young Christian lies to her mother about losing a special pair of shoelaces.
[1. Honesty-Fiction.   2. Conduct of life-Fiction.   3. Christian life-Fiction.]
I. Dorenkamp, Michelle, ill.   II. Title.
PZ7.L5724Sh 1987
[Fic]   87-5267
ISBN 0781432588

To my Lord, Jesus Christ,
the true author of this book
(I only held the pencil)
and
To Dean, my husband
and
To Cara, my nine-year-old coach.

Who may climb the mountain of the Lord and enter where he lives? Who may stand before the Lord? Only those with pure hands and hearts, who do not practice dishonesty and lying. They will receive God's own goodness as their blessing from him, planted in their lives by God himself, their Savior. These are the ones who are allowed to stand before the Lord and worship the God of Jacob.
Psalm 24:3-6
The Living Bible

ACKNOWLEDGMENTS

I want especially to thank Jeanne Rotert for her uplifting prayers and enthusiasm during each phase of the writing of this book.

I am grateful for the careful editing by Julie Smith, for the aid of Bruce Longstreth and Diana Scimone, and for the encouragement of Grace Ketterman.

A special thanks goes to Vicky Bettcher, Karen Nigro, and Toni Buie for sharing their data processing skills with *ALEX*.

Thank you, Ed Marquette, for the many long hours spent reviewing and revising.

Thank you, Lindsay Mayton, for your loving support.

Thank you, Dean, for your patience.

Thank you, Cara, for your inspiration.

Thank You, Jesus.

CONTENTS

CHAPTER 1

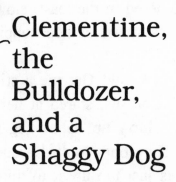

Clementine, the Bulldozer, and a Shaggy Dog

"Hey, come on Alex! We gotta get Clementine outa there!" cried Jason.

Clementine! What a ridiculous name for a turtle, thought Alex. She peered through the fence. "Brussels sprouts!" Alex grumbled. "The last recess of the day, and I'm stuck trying to rescue a stupid turtle!"

"What'd you have to bring dumb old Clementine to school for anyway?" she hollered at Jason.

"I told you already—for show and tell. Now, do something, please!" Jason shrieked back, hopping first on one foot, then on the other.

"Okay," muttered Alex, gazing out of the fence at the turtle. Clementine, who was not bothered in the least, slowly inched through the grass, now and then stopping to crunch a blade of it.

"I know! Get me a stick!" cried Alex.

Jason just stared at her dumbly.

"Hurry up! Get a big stick!"

They both looked around wildly. Jason, who was just too upset to think clearly, picked up a twig. Alex grabbed a more respectable-sized stick and jammed it through a hole in the fence.

"Too short," sighed Alex.

"Oh, no!" wailed Jason. "My turtle! My turtle!" Grabbing hold of the fence with both hands and shaking it as hard as he could, he yelled, "Clementine! You get back here!"

Oh, brussels sprouts, thought Alex. *In a minute, I suppose he'll start bawling like a baby about his old turtle! How did I ever get mixed up with this kindergartner? Ever since he moved in next door to me, he's been following me around at school. Doesn't he know better than to bother a second grader?*

"Hey, wait a minute . . . I know!" Alex suddenly exclaimed. She began pulling off her tennis shoes.

Jason, with tears just starting to run down his face, raised his head hopefully.

Alex was excited. "See, if I tie my shoelace—no, wait—if I tie both shoelaces to the stick and then throw it out, it just might be long enough. Say a prayer, kid. Here goes. . . . Oh, just a second, I gotta throw this thing over the top of the fence."

Alex started climbing the fence but stopped in amazement as she heard Jason say, "Dear Lord Jesus, please bring my turtle back to me."

"Oh, brother!" moaned Alex. "I didn't really mean he should say a prayer. Whoever heard of praying for a dumb old turtle?" She held onto the shoelaces and whirled the stick above her head a few times (just warming up) and flung it over the top of the fence. Perfect aim! What a ball player! The stick crashed right in front of Clementine, scaring the turtle so badly that it immediately turned around and ran back toward the fence.

"Grab her!" shouted Alex.

Jason shot his hand through a hole in the fence and, with a powerful stretch, caught Clementine.

"Got her!" he cried victoriously.

"Stupid turtle," muttered Alex.

"Uh, oh!" Alex gulped. A towering, massive figure in huge black boots stomped toward them, repeatedly blowing sharp blasts on a whistle.

"Double brussels sprouts! It's THE BULL-DOZER! We've had it now!" she gasped.

THE BULLDOZER, whose real name was Mrs. Peppercorn, was Alex's teacher. Alex and her friends called her THE BULLDOZER (behind her back, of course) because of her enormous size and strength.

"Oh, why, oh, why does THE BULLDOZER have to have playground duty today?" Alex could feel the school yard quieting as everyone turned to watch.

"Alexandria Brackenbury! Get off that fence!" ordered Mrs. Peppercorn. "You know you're not supposed to climb this fence! Look at you! You've got mud all over your knees and your shirt's torn. All right! What have you two been doing?"

Alex hearing her heart pounding and feeling her legs quivering, couldn't seem to open her mouth. She could only stare at THE BULLDOZ-ER'S big, black boots. Those boots seemed to get bigger and bigger every second. Jason frantically clutched Clementine behind his back.

"Won't answer me, huh?" said Mrs. Pepper-corn. "Okay, you two follow me! You can spend the rest of your recess standing beside me!" THE BULLDOZER marched off, motioning them to follow at her heels.

Alex took a hurried step, but her foot came right out of her shoe. She felt mud seep into her sock.

"Brussels sprouts," she moaned, "my shoe-laces!" The stick with her laces tied to it was still on the other side of the fence. Should she go back and try to reach her shoelaces? No! Better not. THE BULLDOZER was too mad and would not understand about lost shoelaces. Besides, then she'd have to explain about Clementine, and Jason would probably get in trouble for bringing his turtle outside at recess.

Alex grumbled, "Hide that dumb turtle! THE BULLDOZER would probably make turtle soup outa her!"

Horrified, Jason crammed Clementine into one of his pockets.

Dumb, dumb, dumb, DUMB turtle! Alex's shoes flapped around her feet. Other children giggled at them. Why did kids love to see others in trouble, Alex wondered.

They reached the end of the playground where the teachers always stood and took their places by Mrs. Peppercorn. Alex stood next to her teacher and Jason stood next to Alex.

Alex glanced at Jason. He looked sick! His face was all puffy and red, and he had to keep pushing Clementine's head back down into his pocket. *What a goofy little kid,* she thought. *He's not so bad really. If only he didn't like turtles so much.* She reached over and patted his shoulder.

"Don't worry, Jason. Recess will be over soon," Alex managed to whisper. Jason looked grateful.

Standing beside THE BULLDOZER wasn't much fun, but it gave Alex time to think. "Some recess!" she exclaimed to herself. Well, actually, it had been sort of exciting. She almost giggled out loud as she remembered how funny

14

THE BULLDOZER had looked as she'd stomped up to them, puffing on her whistle!

Of course, she had left her shoelaces on the other side of the fence. She better get them back. Those were her special (and only) laces with little baseballs printed all over them. Brussels sprouts. If she lost them her mother would be mad! They had cost three whole dollars. Well, she could get them after school. She'd just climb the fence. . . . Boy! How about that turtle? Old Clementine had really moved fast when the stick fell in front of her . . . *hmmm* . . . that was right after Jason's prayer. Could that have had anything to do with it?

Alex looked over at Jason and Clementine. "Lord," she whispered, "do You really care about dumb, creepy turtles?"

After school, Alex and her best friend Janie hid behind a row of bushes at the side of the school building. They watched as Jason and Alex's little brother, Rudy, skipped down the sidewalk toward home. The girls planned to rescue Alex's shoelaces and didn't want the younger boys in the way. Alex waited until they were out of sight.

"Let's go!" she whispered to Janie.

The girls raced around the building to the playground.

"Okay," said Alex, "you know what to do, right?"

"Sure," answered Janie. "You climb the fence and then hand the stick with your shoelaces over to me and then you climb back over. Simple!"

"Simple!" echoed Alex. She stopped suddenly. Her feet had walked out of her shoes, and she was standing in the mud.

"Brussels sprouts! This is ridiculous! I'm just going barefoot!" She peeled her soaked socks off, rolled them into a gooey ball, and pushed them into her backpack.

"Your mother isn't going to like that," commented Janie.

"Oh, come on," shrugged Alex. She leaped and hopped the rest of the way to the fence, dodging most of the sharp rocks and missing most of the puddles.

Without waiting for Janie to catch up with her, she began climbing the fence. Ouch! The fence links hurt her bare feet.

Alex, being an excellent fence climber, was up and over before Janie even reached the fence. She only felt her jeans snag once on the spikes at the top.

"Now, where is that stick with my laces on it?" Alex looked carefully at the ground, even getting down on her hands and knees to crawl over the area. "I can't find it!" she shouted in frustration.

Janie, peering through the fence from the other side, said, "Maybe this is the wrong place. I thought you were more up that way. . . . You know, across from the swings."

"Oh," replied Alex, "maybe so." She got up and turned toward the swings. "Oh, no, look!" Alex pointed. A few yards from her was one of the biggest, shaggiest, meanest dogs she had ever seen, and it was heading right toward her. But, worst of all—Alex squinted to get a better look— in his mouth was a stick with two blue shoelaces hanging from it.

"Yikes, what do we do now?" yelled Janie.

"Shhh! You might make him mad if you yell

so loud," Alex whispered.

"He looks mad already," Janie whispered back.

Alex kept close to the fence, trying to figure how fast she could climb back over it *and* how high the dog could leap.

"Well, maybe he just looks mad but he's really friendly," whispered Alex hopefully. The dog had stopped only a few feet away and was staring at them intently.

"I don't think so," warned Janie.

"Janie, I gotta get my shoelaces!" retorted Alex ferociously.

She started inching her way toward the dog. "Nice poochie, will you give me the stick?"

"Ohhh, I can't even look," moaned Janie, covering her eyes.

The "poochie" just stared at Alex.

Brussels sprouts! thought Alex. *He's as big as I am—even bigger! And look at those teeth! Oh, wow! But those teeth are holding the stick with my shoelaces tied on it. Well, maybe he doesn't really care about the stick. Maybe I can get it.*

Alex slowly reached out one hand toward the

dog. "Grrrr," the dog growled, showing even bigger teeth.

Alex jumped back quickly!

"Get outa there!" hissed Janie.

But Alex was determined. "Those are my shoelaces!" she shouted at the dog.

"Grrrr! Ruff! Ruff!" barked the dog. He shook his head from side to side. Janie began screaming. The dog barked even louder and took a couple of steps toward Alex.

Alex, deciding she had been brave enough, leaped to the top of the fence, fully expecting the dog to nip at her toes. But the dog, quite unexpectedly, turned and bounded away. Alex was left, perched on top of the fence, to watch the dog and her shoelaces disappear.

"Brussels sprouts!" Alex was thoroughly disgusted. "Now, how am I going to get my shoelaces back?"

"Get down and let's get out of here!" Janie was thoroughly frightened.

They started for home with Janie in the lead this time. Alex didn't even feel the rocks under her bare feet. She was too upset. Luckily, she remembered to pick up her backpack.

Janie attempted to cheer up her friend. "Well, you tried, you know."

Alex didn't answer.

"Well," Janie tried again. "Your mom will buy you new shoelaces."

Alex only groaned. Her mother would never buy her *baseball* laces again. How would she understand that Alex had lost them trying to save a turtle? No, her mother would *not* understand, especially when Alex got her shoes all wet and muddy. It would have been better if the dog had bitten her in the leg and she had gone to the hospital. Then, *maybe* her mother would have felt so sorry for her that she wouldn't get mad and Alex would get new laces. Brussels sprouts!

CHAPTER 2

The
First
Lie

When the girls reached Alex's house, Janie called "Good luck!" and ran through the backyard. Janie lived right in back of Alex.

"Good luck, phooey," mumbled Alex. Janie could say that. She wasn't the one in all the trouble. Alex paused in front of her front door. *Maybe I shouldn't tell Mom exactly what happened.*

Bam! The door shot forward, knocking Alex to one side. A mass of arms and legs churned down the steps.

"Hey, watch where you're going!" Alex shouted.

"Oh, watch yourself, banana nose!" cried a small, blond-haired boy. This was Alex's little

22

brother, Rudy.

Rudy's real name was David, but he had always called himself "Rudy." Only Rudy (or David) knew why. The other members of the family had given in long ago to the name change. Rudy was five years old and a major source of trouble for Alex.

Now, there he was, with his tongue sticking out of his mouth, jumping and giggling with his friends. One of the friends was Jason. How could Jason stand there and laugh at her when she'd suffered so much because of his yucky turtle? Alex glared at Jason. He quickly lost his smile. Then she turned her frown on Rudy.

"You little goblin! I'm gonna make you into meat loaf!" shrieked Alex. But before she could take even one step, she heard her mother call her.

"Alex! Is that you? You're late from school." Her mother came to the door. "Ignore your brother and come on in. Alex! What in the world has happened to you? And why are you barefoot? It's not that warm. Oh, just look at you!"

Alex looked herself over. "It's just a little mud, Mom. I, uh, fell down at recess."

Her mother was exasperated. "A little mud? You're covered with it. And your shirt's torn and missing a button, and your jeans are ripped!"

"They are?" replied Alex.

"And where are your shoes and why don't you have them on?"

"They're in my backpack," answered Alex, feeling a little exasperated herself. Too many things had gone wrong today, and now there were too many questions.

"Well, go into your bedroom and get out of those clothes. No . . . no, wait, just take them off here in the hallway. I don't need mud all over the house, and you'll have to take a bath right away!"

Alex peeled off her shirt and jeans as her mother reached into her backpack.

"Oooh, yuck!" gasped Mother as she grabbed one of Alex's slimy socks. She then pulled out the other sock and the mud-coated shoes.

"Were you wading in the creek again, Alexandria?" accused Mother. (Her mother only called her "Alexandria" when she was angry.) "I don't think I'll ever get these shoes clean. And, where are the shoelaces?''

Alex had had enough! *Mom believes I've gone in the creek. She's yellin' at me before I can even explain what happened. I was just trying to help my friend get his turtle. She's not being fair. Just for that I won't tell her how I lost my laces!*

"No, I didn't go in the creek," Alex told her mother, "and I, uh, loaned my shoelaces to Janie, uh, 'cause she needed them for gym class and hers broke." LIAR! screamed a voice inside of her. Alex's face felt hot and her legs started shaking strangely, but she didn't correct the lie.

Her mother just looked at her for what seemed like a long time. Then, shrugging her shoulders, Mother gathered up the clothes and walked away.

In the bathtub, Alex scrunched down until the water reached her chin. She was miserable. She hadn't even bothered to make purple bubbles from her giant plastic softball bubble bath container.

Brussels sprouts! I shouldn't have said that to Mom, she thought. Alex couldn't remember ever telling her mother such a straight-out lie. Well, there was the time she'd said that Rudy broke her favorite miniature glass horse. (She'd paid a whole dollar for it at the carnival.) Rudy *had* fallen against her dresser and knocked it off. Of course, Alex had first shoved him into the dresser.

"Maybe I should go tell Mom what really happened," Alex said to herself. "No, I'd just get in more trouble for lying. Anyway, Mom really wasn't very fair. She thought I went into the creek and I didn't!" Alex kicked the water, splashing some out of the tub.

Alex gave the water a couple more good kicks. *So . . . maybe if she thinks I'm so bad*, she thought angrily, *I'll just be bad. But lying is wrong*, she reminded herself. *It's a sin. God won't like it.*

"Oh, I don't know what to do," sighed Alex. She ducked her face under water and blew bubbles.

"Rudy! Sit up straight and quit wiggling," Mother ordered.

"Yes," agreed Father. "The dinner table is not the place to do cartwheels and somersaults."

Rudy giggled, "You mean I shouldn't do this?" He turned upside down in his chair. Father quickly grabbed a kicking foot an inch above the mashed potato bowl.

"I give up," sighed Mother.

Mom says that a lot, thought Alex. *I hope she never really gives up.* Alex wasn't too sure just what her mother meant by "giving up." She didn't want her to give up anything. Unless, of course, it was Rudy.

Dinner was almost over. Roast beef, mashed potatoes, broccoli, and applesauce. What a dull dinner! Alex wondered why they couldn't have something exciting—like hot dogs or pizza.

"Mmmm, this is yummy!" remarked Alex's older sister, Barbara. She daintily spooned another helping of potatoes onto her plate and shaped them into a smooth, miniature mountain. Barbara then made a perfectly round little hole in the top of her mountain. She carefully filled it almost to the top with gravy.

Alex wished that just once her mountain would leak. She sat very still concentrating on Barbara's potato mountain, hoping to see brown juice ooze out the sides. But she was disappointed. It didn't leak.

Miss Perfect! Barbara never does anything wrong. She sure doesn't get into messes like me. I bet she's never told a lie. She's always kind and polite and . . . what does Mom say? Oh, yeah, "mature for her age." Alex wasn't quite sure what that meant. It had something to do with acting grown up. To Alex, Barbara *was* grown up. After all, her sister was twelve and in the sixth grade.

Mom sometimes would ask Alex why she couldn't be more like her sister. Brussels sprouts! How could she be like her sister? She was Alex, not Barbara! Anyway, her sister never did anything exciting. All she wanted to do was wash her hair, talk on the phone, listen to goofy records, and put on that awful, hot pink nail polish.

"Hey, Firecracker!" boomed her father, leaning across the table. "What's the matter? You haven't said two words all through dinner."

Her father always called Alex "Firecracker." He had special nicknames for all his children. He called Barbara "Princess" and he called Rudy

28

"Steam Roller." Alex also had special nick-
names for her brother and sister. She called
Barbara "Miss Mushy" and she called Rudy
"Goblin."

"I have so said two words, Dad," Alex answered. "I've said *more* than two words!"

"Well, excuuuse me," apologized Father. He
made a low bow and pretended to crash his
forehead on the table. Alex had to giggle. Dad
could be so funny!

"Please tell me, my dearest Firecracker,"
asked her father, "what two words did you

favor us with?''

''Well, just awhile ago,'' answered Alex, ''I said 'please pass the butter.' ''

Hoots and hollers of laughter came from her father, mother, and sister.

''Well, what's so funny?'' demanded Alex. ''That's more than two words. That's four words!''

They all laughed again. Alex sighed. *Grown-ups! I'll never understand them.*

After dinner was finally over, Alex ran upstairs to her bedroom and closed the door. She needed a quiet place. She had some thinking to do. Unfortunately, no one else in her family understood.

''Alex! ALEX!'' cried Rudy. ''You wanna race Big Wheels?'' Sometimes, when Alex felt she could stand being around Rudy, they would speed around the driveway on their ''motorcycles.''

She flung open her door. ''No!'' she yelled down the stairway. ''Go away, Goblin!'' She slammed her door shut again.

Her mother immediately opened it. ''Alexandria! There was no reason to yell at your brother like that. That was rude. What is the matter with you tonight?''

"Nothing," Alex told her. She climbed on her bed and hugged her stuffed cat, Garfield.

Mother left the room.

As Alex lay on the bed holding her cat, her thoughts returned to her shoelaces. *What can I do? I gotta have shoelaces.*

Her sister's voice interrupted her thoughts. "Alex! Hey, Alex! Your favorite show's on TV. Don't you want to watch it?''

Alex yanked her door open again. "No, thank you, Miss Mushy," she called sweetly (a little too sweetly). Her mother, who was standing in the upstairs hallway, gave her a frown.

Alex banged her door shut. "How can anyone think around here?" she moaned.

Her door opened again. Thinking it was Barbara, Alex cried, "I don't wanna watch TV! Leave me alone!" Her mother stood in the doorway.

Mother gave Alex a long look. She said quietly, "I've washed your shoes, Alex. Here they are. They're a little wet, but they should dry by morning." Mother turned and left, closing the door softly.

Alex stared at the door for a long time. "I am mean and ugly," she told herself. "I yelled at Mom and I lied to her and I'm afraid to tell her the truth." She slowly sank to the floor. Alex felt guilty.

"Hey, Firecracker!" she heard her father call. Alex didn't feel like getting up.

"FIRECRACKER!" That call was much louder. She had better answer. She didn't need Dad angry with her, too.

Alex sighed and opened her door. Before she could answer, her father called up the stairs. "Janie's on the telephone."

Janie! Oh, good! Talking to her best friend would surely help. Alex rushed into Barbara's room to answer the phone.

"Hello," she said.

"Hi," answered Janie. "Did you tell your mom about your shoelaces? Are you in trouble?"

"Well, not exactly," replied Alex.

"You mean she didn't get mad?"

"No . . . I mean I didn't tell her," Alex stated.

"Oh . . . you mean she didn't even notice?"

Janie sounded surprised.

Alex looked up. Her mother was standing in the doorway.

"Alex," said Mother, "tell Janie not to forget to bring your shoelaces to school tomorrow. You'll need them."

"Uh, okay," said Alex to her mother.

"Alex? Alex, are you still there?" Janie's voice shouted over the telephone.

"Well, tell her right now so you don't forget," suggested Mother.

"Okay! Uh, Janie, my mom says not to forget my shoelaces in the morning!"

"Huh?" asked Janie. "What are you talking about?"

"I said," repeated Alex, "don't forget my shoelaces in the morning!" She glanced at her mother. Mother nodded her head and left the doorway.

"Have you gone crazy?" yelled Janie. "I don't have your laces! The dog has them! Don't you remember?"

Alex hissed into the phone, "Of course, I remember!" She then tried to explain to Janie all that had happened.

Janie was amazed. "You mean you told your mom that you gave your shoelaces to me for my gym class? That's looney! Alex, how could you say that? Now, when you don't have your laces tomorrow she'll blame me!"

"No, she won't," Alex tried to reassure Janie. "Don't worry, I'll think of something."

"Well, you better think of telling her the truth!" snapped Janie and hung up.

Back in her room, Alex slowly undressed and pulled her Incredible-Hulk-holding-up-a-building pajama top over her head. Mother had bought the pajamas especially for her in the boys' department. Alex hated nightgowns. Such silly, sissy things. They didn't even keep your legs warm!

Alex turned out the light and crawled into bed with Garfield.

Pretty soon her door opened and a shadow walked across the room and sat down on the edge of her bed. It was Mother. "Alex, honey, do you feel all right?" she asked.

"Yeah," mumbled Alex.

"You didn't give me a good-night kiss," reminded her mother. She bent over and kissed Alex's forehead. "You know you can always talk to me when something's wrong," Mother suggested gently.

I can't this time, thought Alex, *cuz I lied to you.* But all she said was, "I'm okay."

Mother tried again. "Would you like for me to listen to your prayers?"

"No," replied Alex, "I'd rather say them by myself tonight."

"Okay, sweetheart. Just remember that I love you very much," said her mother and gave her another kiss.

Father strode into the room. "And I love you, too, my little Firecracker. Maybe tomorrow evening you'll say more to me than 'please pass the butter.' " He walked over to her bed and gave Alex a good-night kiss.

After Mother and Father left the room, Alex lay in bed remembering the whole day. She thought about Clementine's rescue and suddenly got an idea. *Maybe if the Lord cares enough to help Jason get his dumb ol' turtle back, well, then maybe He'll help me, too.*

She rolled off her bed and got on her knees. "Dear Lord Jesus," she prayed, "if You're not too mad at me for telling a lie, will You help me get my shoelaces back?"

CHAPTER 3

Cowboy Boot Catastrophe

"Alex! Hurry up! You will be late for school!" called Mother from downstairs.

"Coming!" Alex yelled back. "Ouch!" She winced as she pulled and tugged her old cowboy boots onto her feet. There were just no other shoes to wear. She had scrounged around in her closet and had only found her winter snow boots, her dress shoes, and her cowboy boots.

"Alex! Come on!" Mother sounded frustrated.

Alex bounded down the stairs and landed with a crash at the bottom. *Boy, these boots are sure noisy,* she thought. She grabbed her sweat shirt from a hook and flung open the front door.

"Wait a minute, don't forget your lunch," called Mother.

Alex ran into the kitchen.

"I hope you put your tennis shoes in your backpack," said Mother. "You know you have softball practice after school." She was looking at Alex's feet. "I don't think your coach would appreciate those boots!"

"Oh, yeah," mumbled Alex. She raced back up the stairs.

Thump, thump, thump, crash! She was back down again, hurriedly stuffing her shoes in her backpack.

"I wonder where Janie is?" questioned her mother. "She's usually here by now to walk to school with you."

"Oh," replied Alex, "well, maybe she had to go early or something."

"Hmmmm, maybe," was all Mother said.

Alex quickly kissed her mother good-bye and stumbled down the front steps. "I can't even walk in these boots," Alex complained. She hobbled to the side of her house and peered around the corner at the backyard. No, she didn't see Janie. "Where is she? She can't still be mad, can she? We always walk to school together!

Maybe she's sick. That's it!'' Alex hobbled a little farther down the sidewalk. ''No, Janie's probably not sick. She's probably still mad.'' Alex felt awful. She walked with her head down, staring at the sidewalk.

''Hi!'' a voice suddenly shouted.

''Aaaaah!'' Alex jumped straight in the air.

''I've been waiting here behind this tree for a long time,'' complained Janie. ''Where have you been?''

''I got a late start,'' Alex gulped. ''Boy, I didn't even see you!''

''Well, I was hiding,'' Janie explained. ''I didn't want your mom to see me. . . . You know, cuz of the shoelaces.''

''Oh, yeah, brussels sprouts.''

''Come on, we better get going. We might be late,'' warned Janie. She hurried up the street. Alex limped beside her.

The two girls reached school just as the morning bell started to ring. They clambered up the steps and raced down the hall.

''See you at recess!'' they both called to each other. Janie turned into one room, and Alex raced into the next. Alex slid across the floor and into her desk with a bang just as the bell quit ringing. THE BULLDOZER frowned and stared at her for a full minute.

The room was silent. Alex could hear the birds twittering outside and the clock ticking inside (or was that her heart beating?).

"Alexandria!" growled Mrs. Peppercorn. "Since you are so *eager* to get to school today, perhaps you'd like to be the first one to do a math problem on the blackboard."

Alex groaned and looked at the blackboard. Subtraction! The kind where the ones' column had to borrow from the tens' column. The worst kind!

"Well?" Mrs. Peppercorn tapped her foot.

Alex jumped up and bumped into her desk. A book fell off and crashed to the floor. Alex reached down to pick it up and hit her desk again. A pencil slid off her desk and rolled under it. Alex dove for her pencil, lost her balance and fell on the floor under her desk.

The whole room howled with laugher! It took THE BULLDOZER a long time to quiet the classroom down.

Alex lay on the floor clutching her pencil. She couldn't move. She was frozen with fear.

"Alexandria!" called her teacher. "It will be a little difficult to do your math problem when you are lying *under* a desk!"

"Oh, why can't I just disappear," moaned Alex. She wondered how many seconds it would take to dash across the room and out the door.

Alex risked a glance at her teacher. She was smiling! THE BULLDOZER was actually smiling! Alex sheepishly smiled back and crawled out from under her desk. She stumbled up to the blackboard. Giggles and snickers followed her all the way.

"Ahem," Mrs. Peppercorn cleared her throat and the giggles ceased.

"Alexandria, you may do problem number one. Everyone pay attention! I may call on you to do the next one," Mrs. Peppercorn warned the class.

Eighty-one minus 57. Hmmmm, let's see. I can't subtract 7 from 1. Brussels Sprouts! Why is all this crazy stuff happening to me? . . . Twenty-

four! The answer is 24! She turned and looked at her teacher triumphantly.

"Very good, Alexandria," said Mrs. Peppercorn. "You may take your seat now. Jeffrey, up to the blackboard and answer the second problem."

Alex almost skipped back to her desk. *Wow,* she thought, *THE BULLDOZER told me "very good" and she smiled at me. That's great! Now, if I can just figure out what to do about my shoelaces, this could turn into a good day.*

"BATTER UP!" yelled Mr. Glover. "Alex! This time, for pete's sake, get the ball over the plate!"

"Okay, Coach," Alex yelled back. She was having a lot of trouble with her pitching this afternoon at ball practice. All because of her cowboy boots. She looked down at her feet. Brussels sprouts! Her boots kept slipping in the grass and dirt and throwing her off balance so that her pitches were wild. "I probably can't even outrun Fat Lorraine," she grumbled to herself. Fat Lorraine was the worst player and the slowest runner on the team.

Alex got ready for the next pitch. She made a little slice in the dirt and stomped the heel of her right foot in it. Maybe that would hold it steady. She drew her right arm way back, stepped forward on her left foot, swung her right arm forward, and let the ball go. Her foot didn't slip this time.

"Strike one!" hollered Mr. Glover.

"Way to go," she told herself. She dug her heel in again and threw another pitch.

"Strike two! Good going, Alex!" her coach cried again. "Come on, Sally," he told the batter, "don't just look at the ball!"

Sally looked disgusted. "How was I supposed to know she'd finally throw two good pitches? She's been throwing them over the backstop all day!"

"Very funny," muttered Alex. "I've only thrown three pitches *over* the backstop. These miserable boots!" She caught the ball from the catcher and dug her heel in the same spot. She wound up and stepped forward, but as the ball was leaving her hand, the dirt in front of her right foot gave way. Her foot slipped. The ball flew straight up in the air. It hit the edge of the top of the backstop and came bounding straight back at Alex. She jumped in the air to catch it. The ball hit her fingertips with enough force to tilt her backwards. As she came down from her jump, her boots slipped right out from under her. Alex landed flat on her back in the dirt!

As Alex lay there on her back, she heard Mr. Glover yell, "Strike three!"

She lifted her head. Had Sally really swung at that pitch? Sally had, and it was hard to tell whether their coach was more disgusted with Alex or Sally. He just gazed in amazement at both of them. He finally shook his head and walked off the field. "That's enough for today," he shouted and threw his hands in the air.

Alex yanked her boots off and threw them across the field. Brussels sprouts! She started drawing circles in the dirt. "Those boots have caused me a lot of trouble today," she reflected.

"Alex!" said a loud voice. She looked up to see Mr. Glover striding toward her. He was carrying her boots. He dropped them in the dirt

and squatted down beside her.

"I hope you realize that ball practice is no place for cowboy boots," he said gruffly. Alex nodded.

"Remember," her coach went on, "we've got our first big game coming up on Saturday." He looked at her. Alex nodded again. His voice softened, "You know we're not playing tee ball anymore, and I need my star pitcher in good form." He gave her a pat on the back and walked away.

Alex stood up slowly and brushed the dirt off

her jeans. She turned each boot upside down to pour out the dirt. She pulled them back on her feet, picked her backpack up, and headed for home.

CHAPTER 4

Two More Lies and a Gutter Pipe Lie

When Alex reached her house after ball practice she ran around to the backyard. "If I take my backpack inside with my tennis shoes in it then Mom will see that I still don't have my shoelaces," she told herself. "I better hide it!"

Alex looked around and picked out a small bush in a corner of the yard. She made sure no one was watching her. She quickly stuffed her backpack underneath the bush. Then she darted around to the front of the house and stomped inside.

Her mother was scurrying around in the kitchen, banging lids on pans.

Alex tried sneaking down the hallway and up the stairs to her bedroom.

"Alex?" Mother called from the kitchen.

Darn these noisy boots, Alex thought for at least the one hundredth time that day.

"Yeah?" Alex answered without moving.

Mother came out of the kitchen, wiping her hands on a dish towel. "Alex, how was school today?"

"Okay," answered Alex. She climbed up a couple more steps.

"Well . . . how was ball practice?"

"Okay," sighed Alex. She was certain more questions were coming.

Sure enough, her mother asked another one. "Aren't you going to take your sweat shirt off before going upstairs?"

"Oh, yeah." Alex clattered down the steps and hung her sweat shirt on a hook by the front door.

"Did you wear those boots to ball practice?" exclaimed Mother.

Brussels sprouts! I knew she'd ask that question, thought Alex. *Now what do I do? If I say "yes" then she'll just get mad like the coach.*

"Huh?" Alex asked. Maybe if she waited long enough to answer, something would happen—

like the meat loaf would blow up in the oven and Mom would have to run into the kitchen.

The meat loaf did not blow up, and her mother again asked if she'd worn her boots to ball practice.

"Oh, uh, well, kinda," Alex stammered. "I just wanted to see how they'd work," she quickly added.

"Uh, huh," said Mother, "and how did they work?"

"Terrible!" exclaimed Alex.

"Where are your tennis shoes?"

"In my backpack," Alex said. *So far,* she thought, *I haven't told her another lie. My tennis shoes are in my backpack and I did sorta want to see if I could pitch in my boots.* Still, Alex could feel her face getting hot, and her legs were beginning to quiver. She started moving up the stairs hoping to end the questions. It didn't work.

"Okay," said her mother in an exasperated tone, "your shoes are in your backpack. Now, where is your backpack?"

Brussels sprouts! How do mothers learn to ask all these questions? How can I say I hid it in the backyard under a bush?

Alex turned her head away from her mother and said in a rush, "I left it at school. I'll get it tomorrow." She ran up the stairs, into her bedroom, and slammed her door shut.

After a while, Alex heard her mother call her name. "Come on, Alex, it's time to eat dinner."

"Dinner?" cried Alex. "Isn't it too early for dinner?"

"Not if you want to eat before you go to choir practice," Mother called. "Now, hurry up! Jason's mother is driving all of you to the church tonight, and we don't want to make her wait."

"Okay," sighed Alex. She ran down the stairs. Choir practice. She'd forgotten about that.

At the table, Alex gulped down her dinner, trying to ignore Rudy's silliness.

Soon a car horn beeped from the driveway. "Yahoo! Jason's here!" shouted Rudy. He ran to the door.

"Get your jackets!" cried Mother.

All three children hurried out to the car.

"Rudy! Please quit kicking Janet's chair! Jason, I can't talk when you're talking! Now children, we have a lot of work to do. You know we sing at the church service in two weeks and—eeeeek! Ooooh!'' Mrs. Williams, the choir director, slapped a hand to her chest and pointed at the floor. She quickly backed away from her music stand.

"Hey, look! A turtle!" shouted a boy in the front row.

"Oh, wow! Clementine got out!" cried Jason. He ran to the front of the room to grab his turtle. Clementine was plodding around Mrs. Williams's music stand.

"Jason!" gasped Mrs. Williams. "Is *that* yours? It seemed as if Mrs. Williams would jump on the piano if Clementine got any closer to her.

"A turtle! A turtle!" Total confusion erupted as chairs scraped and banged into each other. Most of the children rushed forward to see Clementine.

Alex was not one of them. She had no desire to meet Clementine again. She stayed in her chair, with her head in her hands, and moaned, "Not that stupid turtle again!"

Rudy, on the other hand, was delighted. "Jason! Ya got any more turtles?" he yelled, dashing to the front of the room.

"Don't step on her!" screamed Jason. One eager boy pushed by another and staggered dangerously close to Clementine. To avoid squishing the turtle, the boy hurtled forward and crashed into the music stand. Music flew everywhere!

Seeing her music fluttering around the room was enough reason for Mrs. Williams to risk getting a little closer to Clementine. She quickly rescued her music and picked up the stand.

Jason grabbed Clementine.

"Children!" Mrs. Williams cried in all the excitement. "Quiet!" The accompanist banged several bass chords on the piano.

"I SAID, 'QUIET!' " yelled Mrs. Williams.

The room full of children slowly settled down. Only a few giggles were heard.

"Jason, I do not appreciate this one bit. Go find a box or something to put that creature in!" ordered Mrs. Williams.

Jason and Clementine hurried out of the room and the choir began rehearsing. Alex turned her

thoughts to her own problems. *I told another lie to Mom today,* she thought sadly. *Brussels sprouts! I just gotta find a way to get more shoelaces. Then everything will be okay and I won't have to lie any—*

"Alex! ALEX!" Mrs. Williams called.

The girl next to Alex nudged her.

"What?" said Alex, raising her head.

"Alex," said Mrs. Williams. "Please join your group over by the piano. We are going to practice our two-part song."

"Oh, yeah, okay," mumbled Alex. She got up

to go to her group. She had to walk sideways through a row of chairs and didn't notice that it was Rudy's row until it was too late. Rudy tripped her!

BANG! CRASH! Alex fell into the next row of chairs. Rudy and his friends howled with laughter.

"GOBLIN!" screeched Alex. She jumped on Rudy, who wasn't fast enough to get out of her way. They both smashed to the floor in a heap.

"ALEX, RUDY!" shouted Mrs. Williams. She rushed over to them. Alex, by now, had Rudy pinned to the floor.

"You ever do that again, Goblin, and I'll squash you into mush!" hissed Alex. She bounced on Rudy's stomach a few times to show him that she meant business.

Mrs. Williams pulled Alex off of Rudy. "Alex and Rudy, stop it this instant! Rudy, get up off the floor."

Mrs. Williams looked from Rudy to Alex. "Don't you know what our Lord says about fighting? If someone hurts you, you should not hurt him back. That would make your actions just as wrong as his."

"The Lord," sulked Alex, "did not have a little brother like Rudy!"

"Alex!" Mrs. Williams exclaimed. "The Bible tells us that Jesus, when He was living on earth, had four little brothers!"

"He did?" Alex cried. "How awful!"

Mrs. Williams chuckled. "If that seems like too many brothers, Alex, think about this. We are all brothers and sisters to Jesus!"

"*All* of us?" Alex replied. "Boy, does He ever have His hands full!"

Everyone laughed.

When all was quiet, Mrs. Williams said, "We are taught in God's Word not to fight even when someone else hurts us." She looked at Rudy. "We are also not supposed to start a fight." Rudy looked down at the floor.

"Tell me, Alex, what did Jesus do when the soldiers nailed Him to the cross?" Mrs. Williams asked. "That must have hurt Him terribly to have nails hammered through His hands and feet."

"Yeah," Alex agreed.

"Did He do anything to those soldiers for

hurting Him?'' Mrs. Williams asked again.

"No," answered Alex.

Mrs. Williams smiled. "You're right, Alex. Jesus didn't hurt the soldiers even though they were hurting Him. But there is something He did do for the soldiers," stated Mrs. Williams. "What was it?"

Alex thought for a moment. "Oh, yeah, I know!" she cried. "Jesus forgave them!"

"Very good! We need to follow Jesus' example and forgive others when they hurt us." Mrs. Williams gave Alex a hug.

After choir practice, Alex lay on her bedroom floor. "I should be getting ready for bed, but Mom will be busy with Rudy for a while. Oh, how I wish I hadn't told another lie today. How am I ever gonna get more shoelaces?" She stared at the ceiling. "What I could do is buy some more laces myself. If I had enough money." Alex knew that she didn't have enough money. She'd spent all that she had on a new pitcher's mitt. Brussels sprouts! Alex went back to staring at the ceiling.

Soon she heard footsteps on the stairway and

then in the upstairs hallway. Her sister's bedroom door opened and then closed. Suddenly, Alex had an idea. She got up and walked over to her sister's room. Alex tapped on the door.

"Yes?" called Barbara.

Alex opened the door and stepped inside. "Miss Mu—I mean Barbara, may I borrow some money from you?" Alex asked in her nicest voice. "I'll pay you back," she added quickly.

"How much?" asked Barbara.

"Three dollars," Alex answered.

"What for?" questioned Barbara.

"Uh, I just need it," Alex stated.

"Not good enough, Squirt," said Barbara. "If you want me to give you three whole dollars, you have to tell me why."

Alex stared at her sister. "I can't tell you. It's a secret."

"Okay, kid, but you won't get the money that way," replied her sister.

Alex stomped her foot. Miss Mushy was being difficult. She just had to get the three dollars. But she couldn't tell the real reason why she needed it. Miss Mushy would just go blab it all to Mom.

Alex thought for a moment.

"Uh," she said, "well, you know Mom's birthday is coming up soon."

"Yeah, it's this Sunday."

It is? thought Alex. *That was soon!* She tried not to look surprised.

"Well?" asked Barbara.

"Well," echoed Alex. "I want to buy a present."

"Is that what you need the three dollars for, Alex?" Barbara asked.

Alex gulped. Another lie? "Yes!" she answered quickly. She couldn't look directly at her sister. Alex had the same awful feeling now as when she had lied to her mother.

Barbara looked at Alex. "Where's all that money you got for your birthday?"

"Spent it on my pitcher's mitt," Alex replied.

"Oh, brother," sighed Barbara.

"But I really need it," explained Alex.

Barbara threw up her hands and grabbed her purse off the bed. She took three dollars out of her billfold and handed them to Alex.

"Thanks!" cried Alex and sprinted out the

bedroom door.

"I want it back, kid, and soon!" Barbara called after her.

Alex skipped all around her room. She felt that her troubles were over. Alone, in bed, she thanked the Lord Jesus for helping her find a way to get some more shoelaces. She thought surely the Lord was helping her—after all, it had been so *easy* to get the three dollars. What did it matter that she had lied to her sister? She would buy new laces tomorrow and then, somehow, find a way to pay back Miss Mushy.

The next morning Alex leaped out of bed early. She pulled on her clothes and picked up her boots. She tiptoed down the stairs in her socks and sneaked quickly out the back door. Outside, she paused to jam her feet into her boots. Oh, ow! They really hurt! "Oh, well, this is the last day I have to wear them," she told herself. She hobbled over to the bush where her backpack was hidden. She looked under the bush. There it was. Right where she had left it. She picked it up. "Why do I need to carry these shoes around all day? I can leave them out here 'til after school.

Then I can bring them inside with the new laces in 'em that I'm gonna buy.''

Alex started to push her shoes back under the bush but then remembered the mean, ugly dog who had stolen her shoelaces. ''Brussels sprouts! I need a safer place to hide them.'' Alex looked around. She noticed the gutter pipe that ran along the edge of the roof and down a corner of the house. ''A perfect hiding place!''

She ran over to the opening. Was it big enough? She peered into it. She grabbed one shoe and, with a few hard pushes, shoved it in and up through the curve in the pipe. Now for the other one. She pushed and shoved with all her might. It finally went in, too. ''I don't think any dog can get 'em out of there,'' she told herself. ''But I better make sure.'' She searched the backyard for just the right-sized rock. She found one and wedged it in front of her shoe. Good job!

Alex left her backpack at the side of the house where she was sure her mother wouldn't see it. She opened the back door and went inside.

Brussels sprouts! Her father was standing right by the door. Had he seen her hiding her shoes outside in the gutter pipe?

"Well, well . . . I wondered who was coming through my door so early this morning. Tell me, Firecracker, were you out for your morning jog?" joked her father.

Alex was too startled to reply. She felt her face turn red.

"Let's see, if not for a jog, perhaps you were doing a bit of early bird watching?" asked her father. "Tell me, did you see any red-tailed fincharookas?"

Alex decided Dad couldn't have seen her hiding her shoes. He would not be joking around so much if he had.

"No, no fincharookas," answered Alex. She felt she had to explain why she'd been outside. "I was just out seeing what kind of day it was—you know, if it was hot or cold," she told him. "I gotta get ready for school now!"

In her rush, Alex didn't really notice that she had lied to her father. Lying was getting easier and easier.

CHAPTER 5

A
Stormy
Lie

After breakfast, Alex grabbed up her backpack from the side of the house and walked down the sidewalk.

Janie was waiting for Alex behind the same tree. "I'll sure be glad when I can come to your house again," she told Alex wistfully.

"After today, you can!" Alex announced joyfully.

"You mean you're finally gonna tell your mom the truth?" Janie asked hopefully. Alex winced. Janie made her feel guilty all over again.

"No!" she shouted at Janie. "I've thought of a way to get new shoelaces!"

Janie stared at her.

"See," Alex explained, "if I buy new laces just like the old ones and put them in my shoes,

Mom will never know the difference!''

Janie looked doubtful. She said, ''New shoe-laces always look cleaner and better than old ones.''

''Oh, I'll just tell Mom that you washed 'em after you borrowed 'em,'' shrugged Alex. She explained how the two of them were going to go to a store after school and buy new shoelaces.

''Ridiculous!'' shouted Janie. ''Alex! How are we going to buy shoelaces ourselves? I've never been to a store by myself.''

''Look,'' she told Janie, ''there's a drugstore two streets down from the school. After school we can run there and buy the laces. It won't take long. It'll be easy!''

Janie was not reassured. ''My mom would kill me if she knew I went to that store by myself.''

''She'll never know. Besides, you won't be by yourself,'' yelled Alex. ''You'll be with me!''

Alex was tired of doing math papers. She'd finished three of them while she was waiting for THE BULLDOZER to call her reading group.

She laid her pencil down on the desk and

looked out the window. Huge black clouds were rolling across the sky. *Oh, yuck,* Alex thought to herself. More rain meant more mud and puddles on the playground and softball field. She thought of the trouble she'd had yesterday trying to pitch in her boots. She didn't even want to think what her coach would say if she showed up in cowboy boots again.

"Reading group one!" shouted Mrs. Peppercorn. The shout made Alex jump in her seat. She scrambled out of her desk and rushed to the reading corner, carrying her reading book. CLUMP, CLUMP, CLUMP went Alex's boots as she hurried to a safe chair (three down from THE BULLDOZER). *I wonder why no one else in this class wears cowboy boots?* She wished that she weren't the only noisy one.

"Alex!" her teacher said sternly, "I hope you brought suitable shoes for gym class."

Brussels sprouts! She had forgotten all about gym class. She stared down at her boots and didn't answer. She knew she couldn't wear boots inside on the gymnasium floor. Well, maybe they would have gym outside today. She glanced out the window. No way! It was blacker than ever. *Looks like it's gonna pour,* thought Alex.

THE BULLDOZER picked the girl to her left to start reading aloud which meant that Alex would be the third one to read. "Better pay attention," she told herself.

Just as the story began, lightning and thunder began outside. Flash! CRASH! Flash! CRASH! *Wow, just like giant fireworks!* thought Alex. The windows were rattling as sheets of rain hit them. The lights flickered.

What a storm! Alex couldn't keep her eyes away from the windows. *I sure hope it clears up after school,* Alex said to herself. *I'll have extra trouble getting Janie to the store in a thunderstorm. Boy, I'm glad I found such a neat hiding place for my shoes. The rain gutter is perfect. . . . No one'll find 'em there. Brussels sprouts!* Alex sat straight up in her chair.

The rain gutter! My shoes will be soaked; maybe even ruined! She groaned out loud. *Well, maybe they won't be ruined,* she told herself. *After all, they always get wet in the washing machine.*

"Alex! ALEX!" Mrs. Peppercorn called.

Alex gazed at her teacher and blinked her eyes. "Huh?" was all she could answer.

"It's your turn to read. Are you back from the galaxies now?" THE BULLDOZER looked annoyed.

"Oh," replied Alex. Her face turned red. She looked at her book. She started reading.

"Alexandria!" Mrs. Peppercorn said sharply. "All the rest of us are on page twenty-two. You may begin at the top of the page." There were giggles.

Brussels, brussels, brussels—Alex's fingers fumbled at the page corners—sprouts! She found page twenty-two and once more began reading.

As children stampeded through hallways, Alex searched frantically for Janie. She caught a glimpse of the front doorway. Someone was standing there in a bright red coat. Janie had a red raincoat. Was that her? Alex pushed and shoved her way to the door.

"Janie!" she cried in relief. She should have known Janie wouldn't leave her. Best friends didn't do that.

"Alex," Janie said nervously, "I still don't think this is such a good idea."

"I gotta get 'em, Janie!" Alex answered.

"But it's pouring down rain!"

"Oh, come on. It's just water." Alex grabbed her friend's hand and pulled her down the steps and headed in the direction of the store.

Suddenly, she heard a very familiar voice calling her name. "Alex! Alex!" Alex looked toward the street. Her mother was leaning out the window of their station wagon, motioning Alex to get in the car. Rudy was already sitting in the front seat of the car.

Alex looked at Janie and Janie looked at Alex. Then they both stood in the middle of the sidewalk and stared at Alex's mother. What was she doing here? Within a few seconds they were completely soaked from the rain, but they were so surprised to see Alex's mother that they couldn't move.

"Alex! Janie! Don't just stand there! Get in the car!" Mother sounded impatient.

Alex hesitated further. What she really wanted to do was dash down the sidewalk to the store. She looked to her right. No, she'd never make it. Mom would catch her. Besides, it was raining so hard she couldn't even see the end of the block.

"Right now!" Mother ordered.

"Brussels sprouts!" Alex pulled Janie to the car and jumped in the backseat. Janie, however, stayed outside.

"I can walk," she told Alex's mother.

"Janie, don't be ridiculous! Get in here!" said Mother in her most stern voice.

Janie quickly got in beside Alex.

Mother faced both of them. "I told your moth-

68

er, Janie, that I would pick you up.'' She gave each of them one of her long looks. Then she said, ''I don't understand why you both just stood out there in the rain! Why didn't you come to the car immediately?'' Mother's voice got louder with each word. She wasn't finished yet.

''Why,'' Mother went on, ''were you two heading in the opposite direction from home?'' She was almost shouting now. Alex rarely saw her mother get so angry.

''Well? Answer me!'' Mother demanded.

Alex and Janie cringed in the backseat. Even Rudy was silent.

Alex knew she had to say something. ''We were going . . . to take a shortcut,'' she said in a small voice. Janie looked at Alex with a surprised face, but she kept still.

''A shortcut?'' exclaimed Mother. ''How can you take a shortcut if you're walking in the wrong direction?''

''I don't know,'' answered Alex. ''We just thought there might be one that way.''

Mother stared at Alex in a way that Alex hadn't seen very often. *She looks like she doesn't believe me,* thought Alex. That hurt! Alex was filled again with guilt.

Her mother finally turned around and started the car. "Well," she said quietly. "I don't know either, Alex. I just don't know!"

The ride home seemed incredibly long. Maybe it was because no one was talking. No one except Rudy and he wasn't really talking—just making weird sounds as he flew his airplane around the car.

They finally reached Janie's house and let her out. They drove around to their own house and pulled into the garage.

As Mother began pulling the garage door down, Alex slipped underneath it and dashed outside.

"Alex!" cried her mother. "What are you doing?"

The door was halfway down so Alex bent over and yelled under it, "I'm going in the backyard for a minute!"

Rudy must have thought that was a great idea. He, too, dashed under the door and outside.

"Rudy!" Mother yelled. She pushed the garage door all the way up again.

"Get in here both of you!" shouted Mother. Rudy was leaping around in the rain, shouting with glee at every thunder crash.

Mother rushed out of the garage, grabbed Rudy's arm and dragged him inside. Alex followed.

"I'm sorry, Mom," she said meekly.

Mother banged the door down. She didn't answer Alex. She just pointed to the door. Alex and Rudy marched up the steps and into the house.

Once inside, Alex expected to be yelled at again, but all her mother said was, "Go upstairs and change your clothes and don't leave your wet clothes in your rooms. Put them in the bathroom."

Alex ran up the stairs ahead of Rudy. She didn't want to wait for him. She ran into her bedroom and flung the door shut. She quickly got out of her wet clothes, took them into the bathroom, and draped them over the tub. She then went back into her room and closed the door. She crawled up on her bed and stared out the window.

Still raining! But the sky didn't look quite so dark. *Maybe it will quit soon and I can check on my shoes. They've been out in that gutter in the rain all day.*

Alex was restless. She did a few somersaults on her bed, then jumped down and started pacing around her room.

"Why did it have to rain today? I could have bought new laces and got my shoes out of the gutter and everything. Brussels sprouts! The rain spoiled it all!" Alex was stomping around her room, now and then kicking at something. "I told Mom another lie in the car today (KICK!) and got in trouble for running out of the garage (KICK!) and all because of this stupid rain! It's (KICK!) all the rain's fault!" She gave her dresser an extra hard kick and hurt her foot. She fell to the floor and moaned, "Why is everything going wrong?"

"BANG! BANG! BANG!" Rudy opened her door and was shooting at her with his water pistol.

"Goblin!" shrieked Alex. "I'll teach you to open my door!" She jumped up and chased Rudy

72

down the hall and into his room. She made a flying leap, tackled her brother, and sat on top of him. Rudy screamed. Alex had her fist in the air, ready to smash his face, when she heard her mother yell, "Children!" from the bottom of the stairs.

The way her mother yelled "Children!" reminded Alex of Mrs. Williams at choir practice Wednesday night. Mrs. Williams had also yelled "Children!" when Alex and Rudy had begun to fight. Now here she was again sitting on top of Rudy.

Mrs. Williams's words flashed through Alex's mind: Jesus didn't hurt the soldiers even though they were hurting Him.

Rudy wriggled and twisted underneath her. *Oh, brussels sprouts!* Alex thought angrily. *I know I'm not supposed to hit him back, but he's such a little brat!*

Several seconds went by. Alex slowly lowered her fist and through clenched teeth whispered, "Goblin, I'd love to clobber you, but I'm not gonna do it. I'm gonna be like the Lord was to the soldiers."

Rudy was too surprised to make any sound at all. He stopped his squirming and lay perfectly still.

Alex rolled off Rudy and collapsed on the floor. She was shaking. Alex thought that was the hardest thing she had ever done.

After a moment, Alex looked at her brother. Rudy was staring at her with wide-open eyes. Alex grinned. "You wanna do something in the playroom, Goblin?"

Rudy's eyes widened even more. He jumped up. "Yeah!" he shouted. He hopped to the doorway.

Alex started to follow but noticed a pile of wet clothes on the floor. "Oh, Rudy!" Alex said disgustedly. She gave her brother an annoyed look and carried the clothes to the bathroom where she hung them next to hers.

"You still gonna play with me?" Rudy asked anxiously.

Alex dried her hands on her jeans. "Come on, Goblin," she sighed.

CHAPTER 6

Fishing for Blue Jeans

"I'm gonna play with Alex!" Rudy joyously announced to Mother as he and Alex made their way to their own special room in the basement.

"That's nice!" answered Mother, looking pleased and surprised.

Alex smiled sweetly at her mother and followed Rudy down to the basement.

A large room filled with toys and not-so-good furniture awaited them. No one but Alex and Rudy used the playroom. Barbara had outgrown it, and their parents avoided it. "It's too dangerous for me," Father always said. "I might get hit by a speed skater or shot by a rocket." That was fine with Alex and Rudy. They loved having a room all to themselves. Alex had even tacked a sign on the wall that read, NO GRONUPS ALOWD.

"You wanna play race cars?" asked Rudy, scurrying around collecting cars from the speedway he had built with blocks.

"Yeah, maybe later," replied Alex. "First, let's warm up with 'jump the furniture.' "

"Okay!" agreed Rudy. This was a favorite game. They each took turns trying to go completely around the room without touching the floor. They had to jump from one piece of furniture to another. The first one to touch the floor was the loser.

Alex was crouched on the sofa ready to spring across to a chair when she noticed her mother passing through the other side of the basement carrying hers and Rudy's wet clothes. Pretty soon she could hear the hum of the washing machine. Mother went back upstairs.

Alex had leaped to the chair, then to the coffee table, over to the sofa, and was getting ready to jump onto the rocking horse when she remembered the three dollars she had left in the pocket of her jeans.

"Brussels sprouts!" she cried and ran to the washing machine.

"You lose!" Rudy shouted triumphantly.

Alex flung the lid of the washer open. All she could see was a swirling mass of soapy bubbles. She stared at the churning water trying to peer through the bubbles. Now and then she could see something dark whirling around. Could it be her blue jeans? It could, or it could be Rudy's or even something else Mom threw in with the load. She had to get her money!

Alex thought for a moment. *I could turn the washer off and get my jeans easily. No, that wouldn't work. I'm sure Mom would notice.* Mom always knew when the washing machine stopped even when no one else knew it was on!

"I won! I won! I won!" Rudy was hopping all around Alex. "Come on, Alex, let's play some more."

"Okay, Goblin, just give me a minute. Why don't you go build a really long race track so we can race our cars? I'll be over in a sec."

Rudy skipped back to the playroom.

I wonder if I can grab my jeans, thought Alex.

She started to reach her hand into the bubbles but then had a better idea. Mom kept long, skinny, round sticks down here somewhere. She used them for macrame. Aha! In a corner, Alex found a whole box of them. She picked out the longest one and carried it back to the washing machine.

Alex began fishing for her blue jeans. The first item she caught with her stick was Rudy's blue jeans. She draped them over the side of the machine. Next, she yanked out her father's old work shirt. She also caught her mother's apron, her own T-shirt, Rudy's flannel shirt, and Barbara's sweat shirt. As they came out, she hung them over the washer's side. But where were her jeans?

Alex stuck her pole in again. Yuck! All she caught was an old sock of Father's. She threw it back in. She climbed up on the washer and peered down into it. Maybe they were on the bottom? Alex jammed the stick way down into the machine. It stuck! She couldn't pull it out! She finally let go of it. The stick, standing straight up in the air, jerked back and forth.

"Funny, Alex! Funny!" laughed Rudy as he

bounded over to see what she was doing. "Uh, oh," he wrinkled his nose and pointed at the floor. Alex, still kneeling on top of the washing machine, leaned over to see why Rudy was pointing.

"Brussels sprouts!" she exclaimed. Water was running down the side of the washer from the clothes she had piled over it. A pool of water was forming on the floor.

Alex was frantic. Somehow she had to find her jeans, get the three dollars out of them, throw all the other dripping clothes back in, and get the stick unstuck from the bottom of the washing machine—all before Mother came back downstairs.

Suddenly, the machine gave a lurch, stopped spinning, and with noisy gurgles all the water rushed out through little holes in the bottom of it. Alex could now see that the stick was stuck in a little hole in the agitator.

"My blue jeans!" shouted Alex. She flung them clear out of the washer.

"Yuck!" cried Rudy, as her wet jeans landed on his stocking feet.

Alex paid no attention to Rudy. She had to work fast. The washer was beginning to fill up with water again. At least it was clear water this time so she could see. Using all her strength, she twisted and jerked the stick until it finally came loose.

Alex leaped off the washing machine, threw the stick down with a clatter, and started shoving all the clothes back into the washer; all except her blue jeans. She grabbed them from the floor and searched her pockets. She found the three soaked dollar bills, then threw her jeans back in the washer and slammed the lid shut.

Still clutching the money, Alex found an old towel and dried the floor with it. She then dried the side of the washing machine. Satisfied that all was normal, Alex threw the wet towel in a corner where Mother wouldn't notice it right away. She unrolled the dollar bills and placed them in Miss Mushy's old dollhouse to dry. Nobody would find them there.

Alex walked over to where Rudy was putting the final touches on his race track. She sat down next to him. Her legs were trembling from all the nervous excitement. She hoped Mother wouldn't notice anything unusual about the washing machine. You never could tell about mothers. They always seemed to find out about the bad stuff kids did.

'Specially my mom, thought Alex. She remembered when she was younger, her mother saying, "Moms have eyes in the back of their heads." For a long time after that, Alex would stare at the back of her mother's head, half afraid of seeing an eyeball peeking out at her from under her mother's hair. Gross!

"Alex! Pick a car to race!"

"Huh? Oh, okay, Goblin. Let's race," answered Alex.

"Alex! Rudy! It's almost time for dinner. Come and wash up," Mother yelled from the top of the basement stairs.

Dinner? Alex was surprised. Had they been playing that long? She hurried up the stairs with Rudy close behind her.

Alex ran to the back door and looked outside. The rain had stopped, and the sun was shining.

She looked behind her. Mother was busy in the kitchen. Barbara was setting the table. Rudy was hopping between the kitchen and the dining room, getting in the way. She didn't see her father. Nobody was watching her. She opened the back door and darted outside. She ran to the rain gutter, expecting to find a pair of drenched tennis shoes.

Instead, the gutter was empty! She lay down on the wet ground and peered up the pipe as far as she could. No tennis shoes! Where were they? Where was the rock she'd stuffed in the pipe? Alex felt frantic again. She started looking all around the outside of the gutter pipe. There was the rock lying a few feet away! She was sure it was the same one. Could it have come loose? Could her shoes have been washed out of the gutter by the rain?

Alex made a quick search of the yard for her shoes. She didn't see them. *I don't think they could have been washed out of the pipe,* thought Alex. She remembered how hard she had to shove to get her shoes up the pipe in the first place. Still, it had been a really hard rain.

Alex carefully searched the whole backyard again. She looked under every bush and tree and along the fence and even on the other side of the fence, but no shoes. It was getting dark. Alex suddenly realized that she had been outside for a long time. Why hadn't anyone called her in for dinner? She was starving! She might as well give up. Her shoes had disappeared.

Alex stepped inside the house. No one was sitting at the dinner table. In fact, it looked as though her sister was carrying the last of the dinner dishes into the kitchen. Her mother was standing at the sink, putting dishes into the dishwasher.

They ate without me! Alex was surprised and a little angry. She'd never missed dinner before! She walked into the kitchen.

"Hi, Alex," said Barbara.

"Oh, hi, Alex," said Mother. She kept rinsing dishes as if nothing were wrong.

Alex didn't quite know what to say. Finally, she asked accusingly, "Did you guys eat dinner already?"

"Why, yes we did," Mother answered in a

cheerful voice.

"Well," Alex stamped her foot. "What am I supposed to eat?"

"Oh, that's right. You weren't here when everyone else was eating dinner," replied Mother. "Let's see. You could fix yourself a peanut butter sandwich."

Alex was shocked! A peanut butter sandwich for dinner? They hadn't even saved her a plate of food? She stared hard at her mother's back for a few angry seconds. Suddenly, tears began to fill Alex's eyes. Brussels sprouts! Nothing was right! Nothing was fair! She flew out of the kitchen and up to her bedroom in a rage.

Alex lay facedown on her bed clutching Garfield. Her tears soaked her pillow. She couldn't stop them from falling. Awful thoughts screamed inside her mind. *Nobody cares about me! Mom doesn't care if I'm hungry! She doesn't love me anymore!* Angry sobs shook her whole body. *Maybe I'll run away! They might be sorry then!* She cried and trembled for a long time.

Slowly—very slowly—Alex's anger turned to sadness. Her thoughts weren't screaming so loudly now, but she was filled with terrible feelings. *Mom shouldn't love me. I lied to her! I'm a horrible person! I feel all alone. No one understands. Oh, somebody please help me! What should I do?*

Alex was certain she had never been this miserable in her whole life. It was like lying at the bottom of a huge pit with nothing but black walls all around her. She couldn't get out of the pit. She couldn't even move—she had no strength left.

It seemed as if she lay at the bottom of that pit for hours. Wait! There was a light up there! Who was making that light! All at once, Alex knew. She lifted her hand up and tried to reach the light. "Lord . . . Jesus," she whispered, "help me."

CHAPTER 7

The Lord's Answer

The first thing Alex saw when she opened her eyes the next morning was a peanut butter sandwich. She stared at it, rubbed the sleep out of her eyes, and stared at it again. A sandwich? Could the tooth fairy have made a mistake? No, no. The tooth fairy didn't bring peanut butter sandwiches! Just to be sure, Alex ran her tongue over her teeth. Nope, no new ones were missing. Oh, well, she was starving. Alex sat up, ripped the plastic wrapper off the sandwich, and ate it in four big bites.

"Good morning," said Mother from the doorway. She smiled at Alex when she saw the empty plastic wrap.

"Good morning," gulped Alex. She gave her mother a sticky smile. "Did you put a peanut butter sandwich by my bed?''

"Yes, I did," Mother replied. "I thought you might be extra hungry this morning. Now hop out of bed. Today is Friday," she added cheerfully.

That filled Alex with gloom. *Oh, yeah, Friday!* Alex used to love Fridays. In fact, she had even loved last Friday. Fridays meant ball practice and no more school until the next week. They meant Saturday was really close and Saturday's ball game. But this Friday would be awful. Brussels sprouts! She had to wear her boots again. Her coach would be furious. THE BULLDOZER would be mad, too. Another day of clomping and stomping. And what about the game tomorrow? A pitcher couldn't wear cowboy boots in a real game!

Alex dragged out of bed and got ready for school. She ate a second breakfast with her family. She didn't feel like joining in their morning chatter. She could think only of her problems.

At school, Alex had trouble concentrating. She worried and worried about ball practice and the game. *What will Mr. Glover do when I show up in cowboy boots again? He might not let me pitch. Maybe I'll skip practice. No, then he for sure won't let me pitch in the game. How did my tennis shoes disappear? What would my parents say if I told them I need another pair of shoes? What if I told them all that's happened . . . the whole truth?*

Brussels sprouts! I'd really get it for all the lies I've told! Maybe I could tell them that a mean kid stole my shoes. No, they'd want to know who he was and call his parents. . . . What if I told them a big dog grabbed my shoes and ran away? No, they wouldn't believe that. What should I do?

All day long these thoughts raced through Alex's mind. Whenever Mrs. Peppercorn asked her a question, Alex couldn't answer. Even at recess the thoughts wouldn't stop. All Alex did was sit on the ground and stare at her feet.

By the end of the day, Alex was exhausted from all her worrying. It hadn't helped a bit and now it was time for ball practice! She stumbled to the softball field in a panic. Never had her feet felt so heavy.

Alex reached the bench by the field. Her coach was busy talking to some teachers.

Maybe he won't notice me, hoped Alex. She yanked her mitt out of her backpack and started toward the pitcher's mound.

Jackie, the team's catcher, noticed her boots and yelled, "Are you crazy, Alex?"

"Clam up!" Alex shouted back. Brussels sprouts! It was just like Jackie to open her big mouth!

Alex drew her arm back, ready for her first warm-up pitch. As her arm began to swing forward, someone shouted, "ALEX!" She jumped. The ball dribbled out of her hand and rolled toward home plate. Slowly she turned and met the frowning eyes of her coach.

They stared at one another. Alex's legs quivered like Jell-O, her face felt hot, and her hands were sweating. Mr. Glover didn't seem to be in much better shape. His face was as red as Rudy's fire engine. His chest rose and fell with each angry breath. Alex thought she could almost see smoke rising out of the top of his head.

He didn't say a word. He just pointed his finger at her and then at the bench. Alex knew what he meant. She was benched! How devastating! The

team's star pitcher was benched! She hung her head and, not looking at anyone, walked off the field.

She heard her coach yell, "Sandy!"

"Brussels sprouts!" moaned Alex, "not Sandy Anderson!" Sandy had been trying all spring to take away Alex's number-one pitching spot. She was a continual headache for Alex. Sandy was constantly asking Mr. Glover if she could pitch instead of Alex. Of course, the coach knew that Alex was better. Still, Sandy was improving.

"Oh, brussels sprouts!" Alex sputtered.

"Tough luck," said a voice next to her.

Alex turned to see who it belonged to. Fat Lorraine! Alex felt even more depressed. Benched with Fat Lorraine! She was thoroughly humiliated. How was it possible that Alex, the best ballplayer, could be sitting next to Fat Lorraine, the worst ballplayer?

Fat Lorraine was smiling shyly at Alex. Then, as if she could guess what Alex was thinking, Fat Lorraine lost her smile and looked at the ground.

Alex turned her head away. She tried to concentrate on ball practice, but a funny thing kept happening. She kept thinking about Fat Lorraine!

Alex glanced quickly to her right. Fat Lorraine was chewing on her fingernails. She looked kind of sad. *It must be terrible to have to sit on this bench most of the time like Fat Lorraine does,* thought Alex. *I wonder if it hurts her feelings to be called "Fat Lorraine"? I wonder if she wishes that she was a good ballplayer?*

Alex was surprised at herself. She had never really paid attention to Fat Lorraine. *Oh, brussels sprouts, I have enough to worry about right now! I'm sitting here when I'm supposed to be out there in the field pitching!*

Alex watched Sandy throw a pitch. "Ball four!" yelled the coach disgustedly.

What am I going to do about tomorrow's game? Should I tell Mom and Dad about my shoelaces and my shoes? Alex wondered. She hunched over and held her head in her hands until practice was over.

"That's it for today! Tomorrow morning we play the Hornets! South Park field. Nine o'clock," Mr. Glover barked.

The bench rocked alarmingly as Fat Lorraine got up. Alex felt that she should say something nice to her.

"See you tomorrow," Alex said. It was all she could think of. Fat Lorraine's face brightened, and she waved good-bye to Alex.

Suddenly a hand gripped Alex's shoulder. She spun around. Her coach towered above her. "I cannot let you pitch tomorrow with those boots on," he growled. He looked at her, waiting for her to answer.

Alex didn't know what to say. Then to her horror, she felt tears spilling down her cheeks.

Choking back sobs, she grabbed up her backpack and started to run home.

When Alex reached her street she slowed down to a walk. She was out of breath, tired, and very miserable. She flopped down under a neighbor's tree and leaned back against its trunk.

How did things get so bad? Alex thought back to the beginning of her troubles. Jason and his dumb turtle had started everything! Brussels sprouts! She felt very sorry for herself.

After sitting awhile and remembering all that had happened to her in the last few days, Alex finally began to be honest with herself. *It's really the lies that are causing the trouble! I wonder how many lies I've told?* Alex began counting them.

Alex remembered telling her mother that Janie had borrowed her shoelaces. That had been the first lie.

The second lie was when she had told her mother that she'd left her backpack at school, when it was really under a bush.

Next, she had lied to her sister by saying she needed three dollars to buy a present for her mother. That was lie number three.

She'd also lied to her father when he had caught her coming in the back door so early yesterday morning. She had told him that she was checking the weather when she'd really been hiding her shoes in the gutter pipe. That was the fourth lie.

She had lied again to her mother in the car when she'd said that she and Janie were going to take a shortcut home in the rain when they had really been heading for the store. Lie number five!

Five lies! Five fingers were spread open on one hand. Alex was amazed. Had she really told five lies?

Tuesday was the day that Clementine got out of the fence and today was Friday. She counted the fingers on her other hand—Tuesday, Wednesday, Thursday, Friday—four days! Five lies in four days! "Plus a lot of other trouble," Alex grumbled. She'd made THE BULLDOZER, her coach, and the gym teacher mad by wearing her boots. She'd made her mother angry several times and had almost broken the washing ma-

chine and had missed dinner last night and . . . .
How could so much trouble start with one little
lie?

Alex laid her head on her knees and sighed,
"One lie seems always to lead to another lie. If I
go on like this, I'll be telling lies my whole life!"

Everything was all wrong. *There must be a way
to get rid of all this trouble and make everything
right again. But how?* wondered Alex.

She looked up and noticed the branches of the
tree above her. They were shaped like a great
umbrella hanging over her. Leaves were fluttering gently with little specks of sunlight flashing
through them. The sky was bright blue with
fluffy clouds. All at once, Alex knew who could
help her. If God could make the branches and the
leaves and the sun and the sky and the clouds,
then for sure He knew how to get a kid out of
trouble!

Right there, under that big tree in her neighbor's yard, Alex got to her knees. "Lord," she
prayed, "I've been messin' up. Please show me
what to do. Amen."

Almost immediately, a thought came to Alex's

mind. It was one that she didn't really like. She tried to push it away and forget it, but it wouldn't go away. No matter how hard she tried to think of something else, her mind kept returning to that one thought. After several minutes of hard thinking, Alex understood.

"I see what You're telling me, Lord," she said silently. "There's only one way out. I have to tell my parents the truth. I have to tell them everything that's happened. If I don't, then this mess will just get bigger."

Alex lay down on the grass and stared up at the sky. "It's gonna be hard to tell Mom and Dad. They'll probably scream and yell and have heart attacks and ground me for a whole year! But that's okay. I just gotta start doing what's right."

Alex was, once again, surprised at herself. She hadn't realized how much she needed to speak the truth. Now that she'd decided to tell the truth, another surprise came. She felt good! She felt happy!

There was, however, one more thing Alex needed to do. She got back on her knees to pray. "Lord Jesus, *help* me to tell Mom and Dad the whole truth. Amen."

Alex felt so good that she skipped the rest of the way home. She wouldn't trade the peace she felt for anything—even if she did get grounded for a whole year!

CHAPTER 8

Alex Tells the Truth

The house seemed empty as Alex, rather timidly, walked through the front hallway. Where was everybody? She had expected her mother to be busily fixing dinner, but the kitchen was empty. There was no sign of Rudy or Barbara. Her father wasn't in his chair reading the paper.

Alex crossed the dining room and then the living room. She turned a corner and stepped down into the family room. There were her parents sitting on the sofa. No one else was around. Alex had a strange feeling that they were waiting for her and that they already knew what she had to tell them.

"Hello, Alex," said her mother in a very quiet voice. "Please close the door."

"Firecracker," said her father, "we have something to talk over with you." He pointed Alex to a chair.

Alex closed the door but she did not sit down. She stood, facing her parents. *I just have to get this over with,* she thought.

"Wait a minute," Alex said. "Please, could I say something first?"

Her father looked surprised and maybe a little relieved. "Why, certainly," he answered gently, "go right ahead."

Alex hesitated. "Well," she finally said. "It's kind of a long something." Her voice sounded cracked and a little squeaky.

"We have all the time you need," Mother replied.

"Okay, uh, you see, well . . . it all started last Tuesday when Jason brought Clementine to school—you know, his turtle—and Clementine's a real fast turtle, and, well, she got outa the fence at recess and Jason was bawlin' and I just had to help get her back, and . . ."

With her heart pounding and her knees shaking, Alex poured out the whole story of the

last four days to Mother and Father. She talked very quickly, as if she couldn't get it out fast enough. While she was talking, Alex felt almost as if she were describing another girl's experiences. It hardly seemed real that all this had happened to her in such a short time.

Her parents never interrupted her story. Their nods and their understanding looks encouraged her to go on. When Alex described in detail the dog with the big teeth, her parents shuddered. When she told of her feelings of despair and guilt, their eyes filled with tears. They even laughed out loud when Alex told about the stick jerking around in the washing machine.

When Alex could think of nothing more to add, she flopped down on the sofa between her parents and looked from one to the other. She spread out her hands. "That's it," she said.

"Ahem," Father cleared his throat. "Well, Firecracker, that's quite a story. Tell me, what have you learned from all these experiences?"

Alex jumped up and then sat down on the floor in front of her parents.

"Oh, that's the neat part!" she exclaimed. "I learned that I was praying the wrong prayer!"

"Huh?" asked both her parents at once.

"Well, before tonight," Alex explained, "I kept asking the Lord to help me get my laces and my shoes back. See, I thought He should help me even though I kept on lying and getting in more trouble.

"But tonight," she continued, "I learned that what He really wanted me to do was to tell the truth. So, I prayed the right prayer. I asked the Lord to help me tell you the truth."

Alex paused and then added, "You know, the

shoes don't seem so important now. I guess what's important is telling the truth.'' She looked up at her parents.

''Alex,'' said her mother, ''you have discovered the wonderful goodness of the Lord. He makes everything turn out for the best when we listen to Him and do what He says.'' Mother's eyes were shining with tears. ''Oh, honey,'' she said, ''you have made us so happy!'' She held out her arms and Alex rushed into them. Father wrapped his arms around both of them and all three held each other tight.

After several minutes, Alex wiggled. ''Dad?'' she whispered.

''Hmmmm?''

''When I first came in here tonight, you said you wanted to talk over something with me,'' said Alex.

''Uh-huh,'' answered Father.

''Well, what is it?'' asked Alex.

''Ahem!'' Father cleared his throat again. He took out a handkerchief and blew his nose. Mother chuckled and grabbed a Kleenex and blew her own nose.

"Well, well, Firecracker, I'll just show you."
Her father walked over to the desk, reached
behind it, and pulled something out from underneath it.

Alex looked. It was a pair of tennis shoes. Her
shoes. Only they didn't look much like her shoes.
She examined them. The blue color was gone.
Instead, they were ugly brown with dark streaks
all over them. They were ripped and the entire
heel of one shoe was torn out. They were so
mangled that Alex couldn't tell which was the
right or left shoe.

"Unbelievable!" gasped Alex, turning her
shoes over and over in her hands.

"You are quite right," said her father. "It was
unbelievable."

"But how did you get them?" exclaimed Alex.
"I searched a long time in the backyard last night
and never found 'em."

"I know that. I was watching you," Father
replied.

Alex drew a breath in sharply. She stared at her
father in amazement. He took the shoes from her
and sat down.

"Let me explain, Firecracker," he said. "Yesterday, oh, about lunchtime, your mother called me at the office. She was frantic! She told me there was a huge waterfall flowing over our back door!"

"A waterfall?" interrupted Alex.

"That's what I said to her. 'A waterfall?' " answered Father. " 'Yes' she insisted, 'hurry up and come look at this.' " Father glanced at Mother and chuckled. "Well," he continued, "being the dutiful husband that I am, I raced home in the pouring rain to check out a waterfall."

"Oh, brother," sighed Mother.

Alex was impatient. Grown-ups always took so long to get to the point. "Was there a waterfall?" she asked.

"Indeed, a regular Niagara Falls poured over the back of our house," answered Father. He paused and looked at Alex.

"I stood in the backyard in the drenching rain with mud oozing into my shoes and studied the situation," stated Father. "As I stood there, I suddenly realized what might be causing this great catastrophe."

"What?" shouted Alex.

Father leaned toward Alex and said in a low voice, "I thought there might be something clogging the gutter pipe!"

"Uh, oh," Alex mumbled.

"So, I investigated, and what did I find? One rock and two shoes crammed up the gutter pipe!"

"Brussels sprouts!" exclaimed Alex. She looked at her father. He didn't seem angry so she asked another question. "But how did that cause a waterfall?"

"Well, Firecracker, when the pipe's clogged up there's nowhere for the water to go, so it spills over the guttering at the top of the house," explained Father. "But what I want to know is how you got your shoes up there in the first place. It took me almost an hour to yank them loose!"

"It wasn't easy," Alex replied. She thought of her father out in that thunderstorm for a whole hour trying to pull her shoes out of the pipe. She looked at him with true remorse.

"I'm sorry, Dad," she apologized.

Alex looked at Mother. *Poor Mom. I've lied to*

her and made her angry and sad. I love them so much.

"I'm sorry, Mom," she offered.

"We know you are truly sorry, Alex," said her mother.

"And we forgive you," added her father. He reached over and patted her back.

Those were the sweetest words Alex had ever heard. She reached for their hands and held them tightly.

"You know something, Firecracker?" asked Father. "I think you were right when you said you prayed the right prayer. Just look what the Lord had me buy you this afternoon!"

He strode over to the desk and again pulled something out from underneath it. It was a box. He handed it to Alex.

Alex ripped the top off the box. She gave a cry of joy! Inside the box was a pair of brand-new *blue* tennis shoes!

"Oh, wow! Oh, wow! Brussels sprouts!" Alex danced around the room. Now she could pitch in tomorrow's game! No more sitting on the bench next to Fat Lorraine! Fat Lorraine? Oh . . . Alex stopped leaping. Her face became serious. "I learned something else today," she told her parents.

"What's that?" asked Mother.

"That some kids are lonely and sad because they're always getting their feelings hurt by other kids. Only the other kids really don't know how much they're hurting them." Alex told her parents how she felt sorry for Fat Lorraine.

"I never thought much about her before," Alex explained. "But at practice I couldn't stop thinking about her!"

"Hmmm, maybe that's the Lord working on you again," suggested Father.

Alex thought for a moment. "Maybe it's good that I had to sit on the bench today! The Lord's sure taught me a lot. And . . . maybe it's good, too, that I lost my laces . . . so that I could learn all this stuff."

Both her parents laughed.

"The Lord turns all things to good—if you obey Him," said Father.

"Well, I know two things for sure," Alex announced. "I'm not gonna lie anymore *and* I'm not gonna call Lorraine 'Fat' anymore!'' She sat down on the floor, yanked her boots off, and began to put on her new tennis shoes. ''Hey!'' yelled Alex, ''there's no laces in these shoes!''

Her new tennis shoes had Velcro straps instead. Alex had never had this kind before. She had always thought they were ugly. She looked up at her father.

''Sorry,'' he shrugged his shoulders, ''they were the only kind in your size.''

Alex stared at him for a moment, then grinned and said, ''Well, at least this way I can't lose my shoelaces! Wait a minute! If these were the only shoes in my size, I bet the Lord wanted me to have this kind so I'd be sure and not lose my laces again!''

All three of them looked at one another and burst into laughter. Alex was sure she could hear the Lord laughing with them.

''What's so funny?'' shrieked a small voice. Rudy had jumped into the room and was glaring at them. ''I'm starving!''

Just then Barbara came trotting around the corner and into the room. ''Sorry,'' she told her parents. "I kept him outside as long as I could."

"I know," said Mother, "and it's okay. We're all finished in here."

"How about pizza for everybody?" Father asked loudly.

Everyone shouted hooray and hurried to get ready to go out to eat.

Alex dashed down to the basement. She had just remembered something she had to do. She ran over to the dollhouse. The three dollar bills were still where she'd left them to dry the day before.

All of a sudden, an ugly thought passed through her mind. *You could keep them and tell Miss Mushy you lost them.* Alex was astonished! How could she even think about telling another lie?

"NO WAY!" she yelled out loud. Alex grabbed the money and ran upstairs.

She found Barbara in the bathroom combing her hair. "Here!" Alex pushed the dollar bills into her sister's hand. "I'm sorry," she said. "I lied to you! I didn't really want the three dollars to buy a present for Mom. I wanted it for something else.'' Alex then ran out the door to the car before Barbara could say a word. She didn't want to have to explain the whole thing to her, too.

CHAPTER 9

Thank You, Jesus

Alex felt stuffed! She had just finished eating two pieces of pepperoni pizza, one piece of sausage pizza, and a half of a piece of canadian bacon pizza.

They were driving home from the restaurant. Father was listening to a baseball game on the radio. Mother was humming softly to herself. Alex was sitting between Rudy and Barbara in the backseat of the car. Rudy was strangely quiet.

Suddenly, Barbara cried, "Stop the car!"

"What?" yelled Father, slamming on the brakes.

"Oh, sorry, Dad, I didn't mean to startle you," answered Barbara quickly. "But would you stop at that shopping center coming up? Please, Dad, only for a minute? I need to get something. I can't tell you what," pleaded Barbara.

Father grumbled but turned the car into the parking lot and pulled into a nearby parking space. He turned and peered at his oldest daughter. "Will this spot do, your majesty?" he asked.

"Just perfect, Dad! Thanks," Barbara assured him. "Come on, Alex."

"Huh?" asked Alex.

"Come on! Hurry up, Alex!" cried Barbara, grinning at her sister.

"Me, too!" shouted Rudy.

"No! Not this time," said Barbara firmly. She pulled Alex out of the car and shut the door quickly.

Alex could hear Rudy's loud wailing as she followed her sister down a sidewalk. Barbara led her inside a small gift shop.

"What's going on?" Alex asked as they stepped through the door.

Barbara didn't answer. She walked over to a counter and motioned Alex to follow.

Brussels sprouts! Alex went over to see what Barbara was staring at.

"There. That's it!" Barbara cried. She pointed

to a tiny blue and white teapot on a shelf among other miniature items.

"That's what?" asked Alex. Miss Mushy was being so mysterious.

"That's the teapot Mom wants for her miniature collection," answered Barbara. "You know, to put in her printer's drawer!"

"Oh," responded Alex. She still didn't understand why Miss Mushy had to drag her in to see a teapot. She looked at Barbara and shrugged her shoulders.

Barbara started to explain, "Well, since tomorrow's Mom's birthday . . ."

"Oh, yeah," Alex interrupted. "Are you going to give that teapot to her?"

"No," replied Barbara, "you are!"

"Me?" Alex exclaimed in surprise. "I can't! I don't have any money." She looked at the price tag stuck on the bottom of the teapot. It read "$3.00."

"Remember the three dollars you gave back to me tonight?" her sister asked.

Alex nodded and looked at the floor. She didn't want to remember *that* three dollars.

"Well," Barbara continued, "I just happen to have it with me." She dug into her purse and held out the money to Alex. "Go on, take it," she urged Alex.

Alex saw the three dollar bills lying in her sister's hand.

"I can't pay you back for a while," said Alex, as she looked up at Barbara.

"I'm not worried about it," Barbara declared with a smile. "Here, you'll need a little extra for tax."

Alex whooped with joy and snatched up the

teapot and the money. She paid for it and then carried the bag carefully back to the car.

Alex and Barbara did not say a word as they climbed into the car. They could only giggle. All Father said was, "Very mysterious!"

Alex leaned against the backseat of the car and grinned. She was so happy! This had turned out to be a good day after all.

She glanced at Barbara. Her sister had done something really neat for her tonight! Maybe she wouldn't call her Miss Mushy so much anymore.

She looked at her parents in the front seat and remembered how loving and understanding they had been when she'd told them about all her lies.

She wiggled her feet in her new tennis shoes. They were bright and sparkling and felt so good on her feet. Tomorrow they would get all dirty at the ball game, but that was okay. Mom would wash them.

Alex thought about what her father had said earlier this evening—about the Lord turning all things to good. "You sure do, Lord," Alex whispered. "Thank You, Jesus, thank You for everything!"

FRENCH FRY FORGIVENESS

Two Alexandrias!

Alex (short for Alexandria) expects to make new friends when she joins the swim team—but she doesn't count on meeting *another* Alexandria! How can she make friends with Alexandria, who pushes her into the pool for no reason?

Alex knows she should forgive Alexandria, but that seems impossible! Is there *anything* Alex can do to win Alexandria's friendship?

Every kid gets into the predicaments that Alex does—ones that start out small and mushroom. Readers will learn from Alex's mistakes and understand that they have the same sources of help that she turns to: A God who loves them and wants to help them, and parents who understand.

Other books in the Alex Series . . .

HOT CHOCOLATE FRIENDSHIP

The worst possible partner!

That's who Alex gets for the biggest project of the school year. She won't have a chance at first place if she has to work with Eric Linden. He's the slowest kid in third grade.

Alex can't understand why he has to be her partner. Is she supposed to share God's love with Eric? Could that be more important than winning first place?

Every kid gets into the predicaments that Alex does—ones that start out small and mushroom. Readers will learn from Alex's mistakes and understand that they have the same sources of help that she turns to: A God who loves them and wants to help them, and parents who understand.

Other books in the Alex Series . . .

1 *Shoelaces and Brussels Sprouts*—It's always better to tell the truth, as Alex learns the hard way.

2 *French Fry Forgiveness*—Sometimes making friends is harder than making enemies.

4 *Peanut Butter and Jelly Secrets*—Obeying her parents (even in little things) beats the awful results of disobeying.